Dedication

To Dina,

You are an inspiration and a truly amazing lady.
With all that you have been through you are still as
strong and determined as ever and full of
positivity.

To Noah,

You are a little ray of sunshine and a
true credit to your family.

Cheryl Lee-White   Jo McFarlane

Grandma

A Children's Cancer Book

Noah was feeling so happy today,
As his grandma was coming to play.
For a month, he hadn't seen her at all,
As Grandma had been away in hospital.

Noah had missed all the fun they had together,
Like bike rides and picnics in nice weather.
He missed how she would play cars with him,
Grandma was sure to always make him grin.

Grandma was due round at half-past ten,
Noah didn't know if he could wait until then.
His excitement he just could not hide,
As he felt warm and happy inside.

Grandma was a very beautiful lady,
With lovely brown hair that was a little wavy.
She always wore a smile as big as could be,
And made everyone around her fill with glee.

Mum had told Noah that she may not look the same,
That he was to be careful as she may be in pain.

Grandma is ill with myeloma cancer you see,
Which is hard for Noah to understand as he's only three.

Suddenly there came a knock at the door,

Down the hallway, Noah tore.

He was excited to see Grandma standing there,

But wait a minute, where was all her hair?

Where had all her beautiful hair gone?
Noah didn't understand what was wrong.
Grandma said, "It's okay my darling, it is still me.
Come here and give me a hug and you'll see."

Grandma bent down and hugged him dearly.
It was still his grandma, he could see that clearly.
She still had her big smile and sweet-smelling perfume,
Noah was happy as he led her to the front room.

Grandma was still ill, which made her tired and weak,
So she couldn't run around and play hide and seek.
At first, this made Noah feel a little bit sad,
But Grandma read to him and that made him glad.

12

Noah and Grandma still had a lovely day,

With kisses and cuddles and fun all the way.

Despite her feeling tired and needing a rest,

Noah still thought seeing Grandma was the best.

The summer sun had all but gone away,

And the cool autumn weather was here to stay.

With the cancer, Grandma's immune system was low.

It meant she would feel every cold wind blow.

Because of her treatment, Grandma's hair was all gone,

So she needed something on her head to put on,

To keep her warm in the cold autumn air,

Something to work as a substitute for hair.

Grandma wrapped her head in a polka dot scarf,

Noah stepped back, stared, then began to laugh!

"Grandma, you look like a pirate with that on,"

Noah said as he burst into a pirate song.

Grandma started laughing
and joined in the fun,

"Yo ho ho, I'm a pirate,"
they'd both sung.

They went on an imaginary
adventure together,

Finding treasure and sailing
through stormy weather.

The fun they'd had gave Grandma a great idea,
That would help to spread some fun and cheer,
Next time she came with a box of funny hats,
And a long silky wig with lots of plaits.

She had a top hat, pirate hat and a Rasta wig,

When these were on, she and Noah did a funny jig.

'Grandma's silly heads,' is what Noah would say,

As with every new hat came a silly game to play.

19

Out of the box, Grandma
picked up a fedora,

She put it on her head and
turned into an explorer.

Off her and Noah went in
search of ancient gold,

Hunting through the
ruined temples of old.

On went a cowboy hat and they were in the wild west,

Noah loved this adventure with Grandma the best.

Across the desert, on their horses, they raced,

When they saw the Outlaws, they gave a good chase.

Grandma put on a navy beret with a pretty white flower,
Then went on an adventure, up the Eiffel Tower.
Grandma enjoyed their visit to Paris in France,
She was glad that with imagination she had the chance.

Although his grandma was still very weak,

That didn't stop them climbing a mountain peak.

With their imagination, they could go anywhere,

Like a crocodile-infested river or flying a plane in the air.

Despite Grandma having been through a lot,

Noah will always love and treasure her no matter what.

She may look different than she did before,

But she is still the same Grandma her family adore.

About the Author

Cheryl Lee-White is an award-winning children's author and best selling poet who lives in Somerset, England, with her partner and 3 daughters.

Writing is her passion and she loves to share this with others through the joy of books.

Where to Find the Author

You can find the author at the following places -

www.cherylleewhite.co.uk - subscribe to the newsletter to download your free activity sheets and free children's short story.

www.facebook.com/cherylleewhiteauthor

www.instagram.com/cherylleewhiteauthor

Other Books By The Author

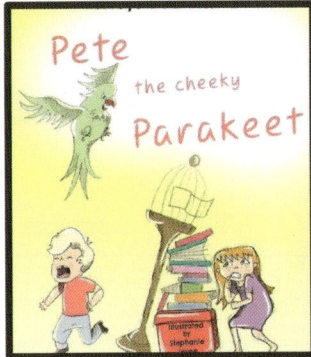

Pete the Cheeky Parakeet

A lighthearted and funny rhyming story teaching children the importance of friendship and kindness.

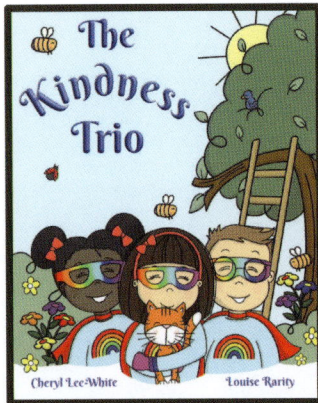

The Kindness Trio

The Kindness Trio, is a children's rhyming picture book that will show children ways they can be kind and help others. The book will also show children the effect being kind has on other people.

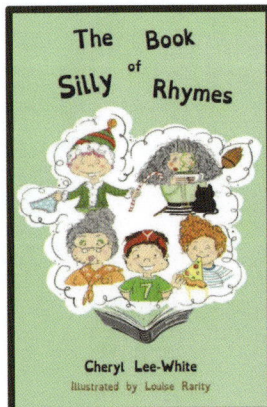

The Book of Silly Rhymes

A collection of short, silly and a little bit rude rhymes for children. Designed for reluctant readers and printed in the open dyslexia font.

Cheryl Lee-White also has a collection of poetry books-

Believe - A book of empowering poetry

Poetry to Inspire and Uplift - poetry to lift your spirits

Thank you for reading!

Printed in Great Britain
by Amazon

39281354R00021